Brigid couldn't escape.

She tried to walk slowly.

"Interesting outfit you're wearing," said Mr. Edsel. "Is that the new fad? Under-shirts?"

"Wel-ll—" said Brigid.

"Here we are!" Mr. Edsel pulled the cafeteria door open.

Two hundred kids were talking and laughing.

Brigid gulped. She stepped inside.

"Brigid!" gasped Jill.

The noise stopped.

Lita's mouth fell open.

Wendy's eyes got big.

"Look, everyone!" said Joe. "Brigid's in her underwear!"

First Stepping Stone Books you will enjoy:

By David A. Adler
(The Houdini Club Magic Mystery series)
Onion Sundaes
Wacky Jacks

By Kathleen Leverich
Brigid Bewitched
Brigid Beware

By Mary Pope Osborne
(The Magic Tree House series)
Pirates Past Noon (#4)
Night of the Ninjas (#5)

By Barbara Park
Junie B. Jones and Her Big Fat Mouth
Junie B. Jones and Some Sneaky Peeky Spying

By Louis Sachar
Marvin Redpost: Is He a Girl?
Marvin Redpost: Alone in His Teacher's House

By Marjorie Weinman Sharmat
Genghis Khan: A Dog Star Is Born
Genghis Khan: Dog-Gone Hollywood

By Jerry Spinelli
Tooter Pepperday

By Camille Yarbrough
Tamika and the Wisdom Rings

Brigid Beware

by Kathleen Leverich

illustrated by Dan Andreasen

A FIRST STEPPING STONE BOOK

Random House 🏠 New York

For Walter

Text copyright © 1995 by Kathleen Leverich.
Illustrations copyright © 1995 by Dan Andreasen.
All rights reserved under International and Pan-American Copyright Conventions.
Published in the United States by Random House, Inc., New York, and simultaneously
in Canada by Random House of Canada Limited, Toronto.

Library of Congress Cataloging-in-Publication Data
Leverich, Kathleen.
Brigid beware / by Kathleen Leverich ; illustrated by Dan Andreasen.
p. cm.
"A First stepping stone book."
SUMMARY: Brigid wants to have a pair of the plastic shoes that all her classmates are
wearing, but her fairy godmother thinks it's better to be a trendsetter.
ISBN 0-679-85429-0 (pbk.) — ISBN 0-679-95429-5 (lib. bdg.)
[1. Clothing and dress—Fiction.   2. Individuality—Fiction.   3. Fairies—Fiction.
4. Schools—Fiction.]   I. Andreasen, Dan., ill.   II. Title.
PZ7.L5744Bp 1995
[Fic]—dc20
94-28614

Manufactured in the United States of America 10 9 8 7 6 5 4 3 2 1

Random House, Inc.   New York, Toronto, London, Sydney, Auckland

Contents

1

Cinderella Shoes

Brigid Thrush sat on her front steps. She looked at her friends' feet.

Jill was wearing them. So was Lita. So was Wendy. They were all wearing Glass Slippers, the Cinderella shoes. Just like the ones on TV.

Glass Slippers were the big new thing at Brigid's school. Everyone had a pair. Everyone but Brigid.

Glass Slippers weren't really made of glass. They were made of plastic. Clear plastic that you could see through.

Jill had gotten a pair a week ago.

Brigid saw them and didn't like them.

1

She thought they were clunky looking.

But then Lita had gotten a pair. And then Wendy. They wore the shoes with brightly colored socks. Or socks with crazy patterns.

You can see our socks through the plastic! they'd say to one another. *Glass Slippers are so great looking! They're so cool.*

Brigid wasn't sure how it happened. But overnight every other kind of shoe turned dopey looking. Overnight Brigid agreed with her friends. Glass Slippers *were* great looking. They *were* cool.

Now Brigid wanted a pair, too.

"When are you getting your Glass Slippers, Brigid?" asked Jill.

"Soon," said Brigid. She pretended to look for burrs on Badboy. Badboy was her dog. He lay on the porch beside her.

Brigid couldn't tell her friends the truth. Every time she asked for a pair of Glass Slippers, her parents said no. They said Glass

2

Slippers were a fad. They said plastic shoes were bad for your feet. They said Brigid already *had* shoes. She'd have to make do.

"You're brave to keep wearing those plain old shoes," said Lita.

Wendy nodded. "I'd be too embarrassed."

Brigid looked at her old shoes. She wasn't brave. She was embarrassed. She'd give anything to wear Glass Slippers. She'd give anything to wear Cinderella shoes like her friends. She thought, If I were Cinderella, I'd have a fairy godmother….

Badboy sprang to his feet. He ran down the porch steps. He stood on the front walk and barked at the house.

"What's wrong with him?" said Wendy.

"It's a cat!" Lita pointed. "Up on the roof."

Badboy hated cats. Even the word *cat* drove him crazy. He kept barking.

They all ran to look.

The cat was giant. Silver. It crouched next to Brigid's bedroom window.

"It's as big as an air conditioner," said Jill.

Brigid stared. She knew that cat. But she couldn't remember from where. That cat had a strange owner.

But Brigid couldn't remember who it was. It was as if someone had locked that part of her brain.

The cat gave Brigid a long look. It leaped from the roof to a tree. Then it ran down the trunk and away.

Badboy stopped barking. He growled once and lay down.

Brigid stared after the cat. She tried to remember—

"Brigid, you still haven't told us," said Wendy. "When will you get your Glass Slippers?"

Brigid blinked. All her friends were looking at her.

"My parents—they're getting me Glass Slippers tonight," she lied.

"Great!" said Lita.

"You'll be one of us again!" said Wendy.

Jill said, "See you tomorrow!"

The three of them went home.

2

The Answer Is No!

"I heard that." Brigid's big brother Gus came out the screen door. He flopped into the porch hammock. "Mom and Dad aren't bringing home any Glass Slippers. Why did you tell your friends they were?"

"I had to," said Brigid. "Everybody has Glass Slippers. I have to get a pair too."

Gus spun the dial on his Walkman. It was clipped to his belt. He nodded toward the front walk. "Here comes Mom. Good luck asking her."

Their mother pushed open the front gate. She carried her briefcase in one hand. She led Brigid's little sister Patience by the other. Her pager hung from her belt.

"Mom," said Brigid. "Can I get a pair of Glass Slippers?"

Her mother shook her head. "We've already been through this. Glass Slippers are a silly fad."

Brigid said, "But everyone else—"

The pager on her mother's belt started to beep.

"The answer is no," said her mother.

She opened the screen door and went inside.

"And that's final!" said Patience. Patience was five. She was cute. She was spoiled. She could imitate their mother perfectly.

"I told you," said Gus.

"But I have to have them!" said Brigid.

Gus shrugged. "Maybe Dad will say yes."

A few minutes later their father pushed open the front gate.

"Wait!" Patience ran to the gate. She checked the security pass that hung from her father's belt. "Pass," she said. She did the same thing every day.

"That is *so corny*," said Gus.

"Dad," said Brigid. "Can I get Glass Slippers?"

"What does your mother say?" he asked.

"The answer is no!" said Patience. *"And that's final."*

Brigid gazed up at her father. *"Pleeease,* Dad?"

"Glass Slippers are a fad," he said. "They're badly made. And unhealthy. The plastic doesn't let your feet breathe."

"If you lose a Glass Slipper, do you have to marry a prince?" said Gus. "If you wear Glass Slippers past midnight, do they turn into pumpkins?"

Brigid scowled. "Very funny. Ha-ha-ha."

Her father patted her shoulder. "A week

ago you thought Glass Slippers were ugly."

Brigid didn't say anything.

"Why follow a silly fad?" said her father. "Why not start a fad of your own?"

"Me?" said Brigid. "How?"

"Wear something unusual to school," said her father. "Something *you* like."

Brigid thought. A long skirt was something she liked. The kind her mother wore when she got dressed up. Red. Swirly.

A tank top was something she liked. The kind high school girls wore. Sleeveless. Lacy.

She'd like to wear a gadget on her belt. A serious gadget. Like Gus's Walkman. Her father's security pass. Her mother's pager.

"Well?" said her father. "Have you thought of anything?"

Brigid frowned. Nobody wore long skirts to her school. Nobody wore tank tops or gadgets on their belts. If Brigid wore any of those things, everyone would laugh. *Brigid looks different!* Dopey *is how Brigid looks!*

Brigid said, "I've thought of Glass Slippers. They're the only thing I want."

"Sorry, Brigid. The answer is no." Her father opened the screen door. He went inside.

Patience went with him.

"I have to have them!" said Brigid. "When I wear my old shoes, everyone points at me."

"If you want Glass Slippers," said Gus, "you'd better do what Cinderella did."

"What's that?" said Brigid.

Gus patted her shoulder. "Find a fairy godmother!"

He grinned and went inside too.

Brigid sighed. "A fairy godmother…"

Badboy stiffened. He sniffed the air as if an enemy were near.

Brigid blinked.

The giant silver cat crouched in a tree across the street. It stared at her.

Badboy saw the cat. He barked.

A fairy godmother! Brigid jumped.

Now she knew where she'd seen that cat! Now she remembered that cat's owner. It was a girl. An unusual girl who had once helped Brigid…

"Take a message," Brigid called to the cat. "I need help again!"

The cat stared at her from across the street. Then it jumped from the tree and ran away.

3

Night Visitor

Late that night Brigid sat up in bed.

A noise had wakened her.

It was a scratching noise outside her window.

Badboy heard it too. He lifted his head and growled.

"Shhh!"

Brigid slid out of bed. She went to the window and pushed back the curtain.

"Ohhh!"

The giant silver cat crouched on the roof. Its tail curled around its body like fog. Its collar of silver bells flashed in the moonlight. Its whiskers twitched.

Sparks seemed to fly from their tips.

The cat stared at Brigid out of huge golden eyes.

Brigid blinked.

There was a silver streak and a tinkle of bells. The cat jumped from the roof to a tree. It vanished into the shadows.

Brigid didn't waste a minute. That cat was a messenger. Brigid knew who had sent it. She crept downstairs. Badboy crept with her. They reached the terrace door. Badboy paced back and forth.

Brigid carefully opened the door.

Badboy bounded outside. He ran to a nearby tree. Brigid followed him. She peered up into the branches.

A girl sat on the lowest branch. She was Brigid's age. She had brown skin. Spindly arms and legs. A French braid. She wore a necklace with silver bells on it. A necklace that looked like a cat's collar.

"Maribel! Maribel Jump!" cried Brigid.

Maribel was more than the cat's owner.
She was more than a girl. She was the one
who had helped Brigid once. Like a fairy
godmother. Then she'd vanished. No one
but Brigid knew about her.

"I knew you'd come," said Brigid. "As soon as I saw your cat!"

"What's this about shoes?" said Maribel.

"*Slippers*," said Brigid. "Glass Slippers." She explained the whole thing.

"What happens if you lose one of those Glass Slippers?" asked Maribel. "Do you have to marry a prince? If you wear them past midnight, do they turn into pumpkins?" She grinned at Badboy.

Badboy stared up at her. He wagged his tail.

"Those are old jokes," said Brigid. "Will you help me? Yes? Or no?"

Maribel leaned back against the tree trunk. "What if I got you the real thing? Slippers like Cinderella's. Made of real glass."

Real glass slippers? thought Brigid. Like Cinderella's? None of her friends had that.

"Well?" said Maribel.

16

Brigid sighed. "I'd stand out in shoes like that. I'd be different. I want the plastic kind. The ordinary kind. The kind everyone else has."

Maribel rolled her eyes. "Why not wear something unusual? Show some nerve!"

Brigid thought of what her father had said. She thought of the long red skirt. The lacy tank top. The gadget to hang from her belt.

"So what if people point at you?" said Maribel. "So what if they laugh?"

Brigid stiffened. The last thing she wanted was people laughing at her.

"I want Glass Slippers," said Brigid. "The plastic kind. The kind everyone else wears."

Maribel shrugged. "If that's what you want."

"I knew you'd help!" said Brigid. "Can I have them now? Can I wear them to school tomorrow?"

Maribel glanced at the stars. She did it the way other people might glance at a clock.

"You mean today," she said. "Do you have gym?"

Brigid nodded.

"Leave your clothes in your locker as usual," said Maribel. "After gym you'll find Glass Slippers there."

"Oh, boy!" Brigid turned to go.

"Wait," said Maribel. "What's your locker combination?"

Brigid said, "Left twenty-three. Right two. Left nine. But don't tell anyone else!"

"Listen carefully," said Maribel. "Wear the Glass Slippers during school. But have them back in your locker by three P.M."

"Or they'll turn into pumpkins?" said Brigid.

Maribel shook her head. "You'll turn into a mouse."

4

Double-Cross

The next morning Brigid walked quickly to school.

She wore brown pants. She wore a white T-shirt. She wore plain old brown shoes. She also wore her red and gold lightning-bolt socks.

The socks didn't look like much now. But they'd look great when she put on her Glass Slippers!

In the front hall Brigid saw Wendy. Wendy wore green and blue striped socks under her Glass Slippers.

"Brigid!" said Wendy. "I thought you were getting Glass Slippers."

"I am," said Brigid. "After gym."

She hurried into her classroom.

"Hi, Brigid," said Lita.

Brigid turned.

Lita wore red socks with purple stars under her Glass Slippers.

"What happened to your Glass Slippers?" said Lita.

"Someone's dropping them off," said Brigid. "During gym."

At eleven o'clock the bell rang for gym.

"Oh, boy!" said Brigid. She hurried to the locker room. She took off her brown pants. She took off her white T-shirt. She took off her old brown shoes. And her lightning-bolt socks.

She put on white socks. She put on her gym suit and sneakers. She picked up all her clothes and stuffed them into her locker. She put her old brown shoes on top.

"Hi, Brigid!" said Jill.

Jill wore skin-colored socks under her Glass Slippers. The sock feet looked like real feet. They had pink painted toenails. "You told me you'd have Glass Slippers today."

"I'll have them." Brigid shut her locker. She clamped on the lock and spun the dial. "After gym."

Brigid ran out of the locker room. She crossed her fingers. "Please, Maribel, don't forget!"

During gym Brigid couldn't stop thinking about Glass Slippers. How it would feel to step into them. How it would feel to walk in them.

Jill would say, *Great Glass Slippers!*

Wendy would say, *You're one of us again!*

Brigid was so excited she scored three goals. Twice she stopped the other team from scoring.

"Nice save!" said Ms. Bluff, the gym teacher. "Brigid's team wins. Everyone inside and change."

Brigid ran to the locker room. She was so excited she could hardly breathe. She reached her locker and spun the dial.

Left twenty-three. Right two. Left nine.

She took off the lock and opened the door. She peered inside.

Something new lay in the darkness. Something that glowed.

Brigid let out a sigh.

Glass Slippers. A beautiful pair.

Brigid put the Glass Slippers on the floor. She yanked off her gym suit. She yanked off her gym socks.

She pulled on her lightning-bolt socks. And her white T-shirt. She reached for her brown pants—

She stared. "What's *this?*"

Jill looked. "What's what?"

Brigid clapped a hand over her mouth. She hadn't meant to cry out. She quickly shut her locker door. She couldn't let Jill see.

"I said—I said—" Brigid tried to think of something. "What time is it?"

The lunch bell rang.

"Lunchtime!" said Jill. "Want me to wait?"

Brigid's hands felt clammy. Her forehead felt damp. "No, thanks," she said. "You go ahead."

"See you in the cafeteria." Jill pointed. "Hey, nice Glass Slippers!"

Brigid waited until everyone left. She opened her locker door. She peered inside.

Her brown pants were gone. Something else lay there. A bright red something.

Brigid pulled it from the locker. She unfolded it.

It was a long skirt. The kind of dress-up skirt Brigid's mother sometimes wore. The

kind of skirt Brigid had thought she'd like to wear.

The skirt had gold stripes. Silver bells hung from its hem. The kind of bells a cat wore on a collar. Or a fairy godmother wore on a necklace.

A double-crossing fairy godmother.

"Maribel!" cried Brigid. "Give back my pants!"

"Who's that?" Ms. Bluff stuck her head in the door. "Still in your underwear, Brigid? Get yourself dressed and over to the cafeteria. On the double."

Brigid swallowed hard.

She had two choices. She could go to lunch in the awful skirt. Or she could go to lunch in her underpants.

Brigid put on the long red skirt. She went.

5

Standing Out

Brigid crept down the hall. She walked as smoothly as she could. The bells on her skirt jingled anyway. The gold stripes flashed.

Brigid would have liked wearing the skirt at home. She would have felt beautiful. Grown-up. But here at school…

Brigid thought, I look weird!

The Glass Slippers didn't help a bit. Brigid knew they were there. But no one else would. The long skirt covered them.

Brigid headed for the supply room. She could hide there. At 2:45 school would be over. The halls would be empty. She'd meet

Maribel. She'd give back the Glass Slippers. Maribel would give back her brown pants.

Brigid crept past the principal's office.

The bells on her skirt jingled.

"Who's that?" said someone.

Brigid froze.

"Is that Brigid? Brigid Thrush?"

Brigid knew that voice. It was Mrs. Early, the principal.

"What are you doing here?" asked Mrs. Early. "You should be at lunch. Come. I'll walk you."

Brigid said, "But—"

"No buts." Mrs. Early was nice but strict. Brigid couldn't escape. She sighed and started to walk. The skirt bells jingled.

"That's quite an outfit," said Mrs. Early. "It's good to see a student with nerve."

"Nerve?" said Brigid.

"The nerve to stand out," said Mrs. Early. "The nerve to look different. If I see

one more pair of Glass Slippers, I'll scream.
Here we are."

Mrs. Early held the cafeteria door open.

Brigid gritted her teeth. She stepped
inside.

All the kids looked up from their lunch.
They stared.

Brigid heard whispers.

What's she wearing?

She heard snickers.

She looks like a fortune-teller!

She heard giggles.

Hey, Brigid, check your calendar. This isn't Halloween!

If you're there, Maribel, thought Brigid, make me invisible! Please.

Maribel didn't.

Maribel met Brigid in the locker room at three P.M. She gave Brigid back her old brown shoes. She gave Brigid back her brown pants. She couldn't understand why Brigid was so upset.

"You got your Glass Slippers," she said. "The skirt was extra. I threw it in for fun."

"*Fun?*" said Brigid.

Maribel held up the red skirt. "You like your mother's long skirt. I thought you'd like this. It matches your socks."

"No one could see my socks!" said Brigid. "No one could see my Glass Slippers. All anyone could see was that red skirt. And my red face."

Maribel stuffed the Glass Slippers and jingly skirt into her silver backpack.

"Heyyy—" said Brigid. "How did you know about my mother's skirt?"

"I know everything about you." Maribel looked her in the eye. "That's my job."

"Your job?" Brigid stared at Maribel. She saw a silver cat with golden eyes. Its whiskers twitched and sparked.

Brigid closed her eyes and shook her head. She opened her eyes. Maribel looked like herself.

"I'll tell you what," said Maribel. "Since this didn't work out, I'll bring back the Glass Slippers tomorrow. Same time. Same place."

"I don't have gym tomorrow." Brigid rubbed her eyes. How had Maribel done that? "I have gym the day after tomorrow."

Maribel picked up the backpack. She headed for the door that led to the field.

She called over her shoulder, "The day after tomorrow, then."

"Okay, but no more 'extras!'" said Brigid. "No more fortune-teller skirts. Leave my pants alone."

The door slammed shut.

Brigid ran to it. She yanked it open. "No crazy skirt! Leave my pants!"

But Maribel wasn't there.

6

Underwear

The next day Brigid wore black pants to school. She wore a gray T-shirt. She wore gray socks with yellow lightning bolts. And her old brown shoes.

Wendy stopped her in the hall. Wendy wore purple and green checked socks under her Glass Slippers.

"Hey, Brigid, you look almost normal today." She grinned. "Where's your long red skirt?"

Brigid went into her classroom.

Lita stopped by her desk. Lita wore orange and blue striped socks under her Glass Slippers.

"Hey, Brigid, where are your bells?" She grinned. "You don't jingle today."

The next day Brigid wore blue pants to school. She wore a blue T-shirt. She wore blue socks with red stars. And her old brown shoes.

Wendy saw her in the hall. "You're still wearing plain old shoes? I feel sorry for you."

Lita saw her in the classroom. "Plain old shoes? Too bad."

At gym Jill walked into the locker room. She looked at Brigid's old brown shoes. She shook her head. "Poor you."

"Wait until after gym!" said Brigid.

"After gym?" Jill blinked. "What happens then?"

Brigid thought for a minute. What if Maribel didn't leave the Glass Slippers? What if she left something else?

"Just wait," she mumbled.

During gym Brigid couldn't stop worrying. She was so nervous she missed two easy goals. She let the other team score twice.

"Brigid's team loses," said Ms. Bluff. "Everyone inside and change."

Brigid walked slowly into the locker room. She was so tense she could hardly breathe. She waited until everyone else was dressed. When they left, she spun the dial on her lock.

Left twenty-three. Right two. Left nine.

She took off the lock and opened the door. She peered inside.

There in the darkness lay...Glass Slippers! Under them lay...Brigid's blue pants!

Brigid let out a sigh of relief.

She yanked off her gym suit. She yanked off her gym socks. She pulled on her star socks. And her blue pants.

Brigid stepped into the Glass Slippers.
She reached for her blue T-shirt—

"Oh, no!"

The blue T-shirt wasn't there.

Brigid searched the floor. She searched
the bench.

No T-shirt!

She caught sight of herself in the locker-
room mirror. A girl in a white undershirt

with pink flowers looked back.

The undershirt looked like a tank top. It was lacy. It was sleeveless. It was like the tank tops high school girls wore.

But the girl in the mirror didn't look like a high school girl. She looked like a nine-year-old who had forgotten to get dressed.

"Maribel!" cried Brigid.

Ms. Bluff stuck her head in the door. "Late again, Brigid? Get going to lunch."

Brigid cleared her throat. "Can I just—"

"No, you can't," said Ms. Bluff. "Go."

Brigid sighed. She started for the door.

Ms. Bluff shook her head. "You children have the oddest taste in clothes!"

7

Brigid, Get Dressed!

Brigid crept down the empty hall. Her undershirt was drafty. Goose bumps covered her arms.

This is worse than the skirt! she thought. A million times worse. The Glass Slippers don't help. No one who sees me will look at my feet!

Brigid headed for the supply room. She didn't pass the principal's office. She took the long way. The safer way. The way past the nurse's room.

Lunch smells filled the hall. Spaghetti with tomato sauce. Roast turkey.

Brigid's stomach rumbled. She hadn't

played well in gym. But she had played hard. She was hungry.

But not even spaghetti could get her into the cafeteria. Not even turkey could make her stand in the lunch line. Not dressed this way. *Un*dressed.

She crept on.

Brigid reached the supply room. She opened the door.

"Is that Brigid?" said someone behind her.

Brigid froze.

"You should be in the cafeteria. Eating."

Brigid knew that voice. It was Mr. Edsel, the school nurse.

Brigid turned. "I'm not hungry. Really."

Her stomach rumbled like thunder.

"Nonsense." Mr. Edsel took her by the shoulders. He steered her down the hall. "A good lunch is what you need. I'll walk you."

Brigid couldn't escape. She tried to walk slowly.

"Interesting outfit you're wearing," said Mr. Edsel. "Is that the new fad? Undershirts?"

"Wel-ll—" said Brigid.

"Here we are!" Mr. Edsel pulled the cafeteria door open.

Two hundred kids were talking and laughing.

Brigid gulped. She stepped inside.

"Brigid!" gasped Jill.

The noise stopped.

Lita's mouth fell open.

Wendy's eyes got big.

"Look, everyone!" said Joe. "Brigid's in her underwear!"

Brigid's face got hot. She thought, Maribel, get me out of this! Please!

Maribel didn't.

Maribel met Brigid in the locker room at three P.M. She couldn't understand why

Brigid was so upset. "You got your Glass Slippers. You wore your pants."

"I wore my *undershirt!*" said Brigid. "Give me back my clothes!"

Maribel gave back Brigid's old brown shoes. She gave back Brigid's blue T-shirt.

The T-shirt was covered with silver stuff. "What's all this?" said Brigid.

Maribel glanced at it. She shrugged. "Looks like cat hair."

Brigid frowned. But she put on the T-shirt. "Everyone saw me in my undershirt! Even the boys. Everyone laughed."

"You got their attention," said Maribel. "You stood out."

"I don't want to stand out!" said Brigid. "I want to fit in. I want to be just like everyone else."

"Sounds dull to me," said Maribel. She stuffed the Glass Slippers into her backpack. "But I'll tell you what. I'll bring back the

Glass Slippers one more time. On Monday."

Brigid chewed her lip. She wanted the Glass Slippers. But she didn't want any more tricks. "Will you leave *all* my other clothes? Will you take *only* my shoes and leave the Glass Slippers?"

Maribel drew an invisible X on her chest. "Cross my heart."

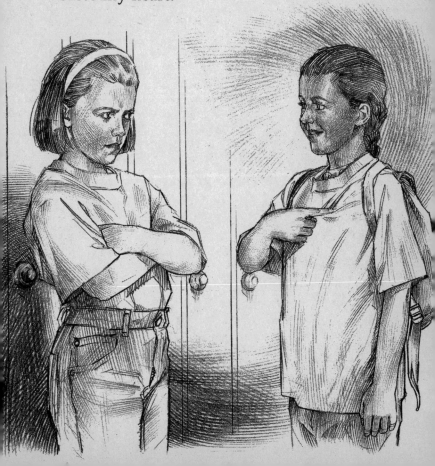

Brigid slowly nodded. "Okay."

"Great!" Maribel lifted her backpack. She opened the door and left.

The locker room was quiet.

Only then did Brigid wonder. Do fairy godmothers *have* hearts?

8

Fitting In

After her awful day, Brigid was glad to get home. But things weren't any better there.

Gus stopped her as she walked in the door. "Hey, Brigid. I heard you've been dressing up at school. And *un*dressing! Is that true?"

"I don't want to talk about it," said Brigid.

Patience ran into the hall. "Dressing up? Can I dress up too?"

"No," said Brigid. "You can't." She stomped upstairs.

Badboy lay at the top of the stairs. He looked at Brigid. He started to bark.

"What's wrong with you?" said Brigid.

"He doesn't like grouches!" yelled Gus.

"Brigid the Grouch!" yelled Patience.

Brigid stomped into her room. She slammed the door. She kicked off her old shoes and rubbed her feet.

She had a blister on her heel. She had another blister on her big toe. Her parents had been right. Glass Slippers weren't good for your feet.

Brigid threw herself on the bed. She wished Maribel were a better fairy godmother. An ordinary fairy godmother. With a magic wand. Most of all, Brigid wished she could trust her.

She thought, I should never have told Maribel my lock combination! Maybe I can get a new lock. Before gym on Monday.

"Brigid!" her mother called. "Dinner."

Brigid slid off her bed. She trudged downstairs and sat at her place.

Badboy growled under the table.

"What's wrong with him?" asked her father.

"Brigid's what's wrong," said Gus.

Patience said, "Badboy doesn't like grouches."

"Now, now," said their mother. "Gus, take off those headphones at the table."

She turned to Brigid. "You were in your room a long time."

"I was tired," said Brigid. "I had a hard day at school." She reached for her napkin. It was where her glass should have been. She reached for her fork. It was upside down beside her knife.

"Who set the table?" asked Brigid.

"You were supposed to set it," said Patience. "But Dad said I could. Because you were in your room. Being a grouch."

"Patience." Their mother gave her a stop-it-at-once look.

Patience rolled her eyes. She flopped back in her chair.

Brigid's father said, "You haven't mentioned those plastic shoes again, Brigid."

"Glass Slippers," said Gus.

"Cinderella shoes," said Patience.

"Not since Monday," said her mother.

"I know why she hasn't mentioned them," said Gus. "She's been too busy dressing up."

"Dressing up?" said Brigid's mother.

"At school," said Gus. "Brigid's been wearing crazy outfits to get attention. To make up for not having Glass Slippers like her friends."

"Is this true, Brigid?" said her father. "Have you been dressing up?"

"Wel-ll—" said Brigid.

"What's that all over your T-shirt?" asked her mother.

"Looks like hair," said Gus. He lifted a bit from Brigid's shirt. "Silver hair. From a cat."

Badboy sprang to his feet and barked.

"*That's* why Badboy's been growling at Brigid," said Patience. "He thinks she's a cat!"

Badboy barked louder.

"Brigid," said her father. "How did you get yourself covered with ca— with *animal* hair?"

Brigid squirmed. She didn't know what to say.

"Does this have anything to do with your dressing up?" said her father. "Does this have anything to do with those plastic shoes?"

"Wel-ll…" Brigid stared at her plate. She
wanted to tell her parents about the bad
time she'd had. She wanted to tell about the
long skirt and the undershirt. About how
everyone had pointed and laughed.

Brigid wanted to tell, but she couldn't.

Not without telling about Maribel. Brigid
didn't want to tell about her.

"The cat hair *might* have to do with
Glass Slippers," she said. "The dressing up
might, too."

Her mother looked at her father.

"Brigid, you've tried hard to get along without those shoes," said her father. "You haven't begged. You haven't complained. We're proud of you."

"We don't want you to follow fads," said her mother. "We want you to dress for yourself."

"But what we want most," said her father, "is to see you happy."

Brigid couldn't believe her ears.

"It's hard not to go along with the crowd," said her mother. "It's hard to be different."

"We still think Glass Slippers are silly," said her father. "But tomorrow we'll go to the shoe store. We'll get you a pair."

"Oh, boy!" said Brigid. Then she thought, Maribel. Monday. Gym!

Maribel had crossed her heart. But did that count? Who knew what Maribel might leave in Brigid's locker? Who knew what she might take?

Brigid turned to her parents. "Can we go to the hardware store, too? For a new combination lock? I need one. Badly."

9

Ordinary Clothes

On Monday morning Brigid put on her blue skirt. She put on her white T-shirt. She put on her orange socks with green lightning bolts.

She took her new Glass Slippers out of their box. She slipped them on.

They felt uncomfortable. But Brigid smiled anyway. She finally looked like everyone else.

Maribel's not going to mess up this outfit! thought Brigid.

She picked up her new lock. It felt smooth and heavy. Its silver case flashed in the light. She spun the dial. The lock sprang open.

Brigid had an idea. She clipped the lock to one of her belt loops. She looked in the mirror again. The lock hung at her waist. It looked as important as her mother's pager. As official as her father's security pass. It felt as heavy as Gus's Walkman. Brigid loved it.

But the other kids would see it and laugh. She unclipped the lock. She'd carry it instead. She left for school.

The Glass Slippers were hard to walk in. The fronts pinched. The backs slipped off. Brigid had to curl her toes to keep them on. She had to walk slowly. More slowly. More slowly still. So slowly that she arrived at school late.

Brigid limped into her classroom.

The teacher, Mr. Gore, frowned at her.

"I'm sorry I'm late," said Brigid. "I have new shoes. They're hard to walk in." She hoped everyone would notice her Glass Slippers.

"Sit down and let's get to work," said Mr. Gore.

Brigid sat. She glanced at her friends.

She stared.

Jill wore a long skirt. It was yellow and crinkly. She didn't look at all embarrassed.

Lita wore a lacy undershirt. It was white with blue flowers. She didn't look embarrassed, either.

Wendy wore a striped undershirt. And a long green skirt. She looked proud and pleased.

Brigid dropped her pencil on purpose. She bent to get it. She looked at her friends' feet.

Not one of them wore Glass Slippers.

All of them wore plain old shoes.

At eleven A.M. the bell rang for gym.

Brigid headed into the hall with her friends.

She said, "That's a nice undershirt, Lita."

"I looked for one with pink flowers. Like yours," said Lita. "The store didn't have one."

"I looked for a skirt with bells like Brigid's," said Jill. "The store didn't have one. Where did you get yours?"

"Mine?" said Brigid.

"Brigid won't tell," said Wendy. "She'll keep it a secret. So she'll always have new, different stuff."

"Speaking of different stuff," said Jill. "Why are you wearing ordinary clothes, Brigid?"

"Yes," said Lita. "Why?"

Brigid pointed to her feet. "Look at these!"

"Glass Slippers?" said Jill.

"Big deal," said Lita.

"Stop kidding us," said Wendy. "Glass Slippers are old."

Brigid looked around. Wendy was right. Not one girl in the crowded hall wore Glass Slippers. Everyone wore a long skirt. Or a fancy undershirt. Or both. Everyone but Brigid.

Mrs. Early leaned out of her office. She looked at everyone in their new outfits. "Brigid, promise me," she said. "The next time you start a fad, make it sensible!"

Brigid reached the locker room.

Ms. Bluff stood at the door. "Where's your fancy undershirt, Brigid?"

Brigid swallowed hard. Her undershirt today was an old one. Plain. Grayish white. With holes. She couldn't let anyone see *it*. She hurried to change into her gym clothes.

Brigid left her old clothes in the locker. She left her new lock in the locker. She clamped on the old lock. And then she made a wish.

Please, Maribel! Change the clothes in my locker. For the long red skirt. Or the lacy undershirt. Do it before I come back!

While she played on the field, Brigid kept wishing.

Please, Maribel. I'll be your best friend. Maribel, do it or else!

She kicked the ball.

"Goal!" yelled Ms. Bluff. "That makes three goals for you, Brigid. You're playing hard today."

Brigid blinked. "I am?" She looked around.

"Are you in a trance?" said Ms. Bluff. "Your team wins. Everyone inside and change."

Brigid ran to the locker room. She spun her combination lock. Left twenty-three. Right two. Left nine.

She took a deep breath and opened the locker. She peered inside.

Her Glass Slippers were there with her lightning-bolt socks. So were her blue skirt, white T-shirt, and new lock. Nothing else.

Except for one thing. A note written in silver ink.

Sorry, Brigid. But I crossed my heart.

M. Jump

10

The Next Big Thing

That afternoon Brigid walked home with her friends. She limped a little. The Glass Slippers pinched her toes. They slipped off her heels. Her parents had been right. They were dopey shoes. She'd never wear them again.

Brigid sighed. Her parents wouldn't let her go along with another fad. Ever.

"Come on, Brigid," said Wendy.

Brigid gritted her teeth and tried to speed up. She gripped her new lock harder. That helped her feet hurt less.

She liked the way the lock fit in her hand. It felt cool. Smooth. Heavy. When she spun the dial, it made a deep clicking sound.

Brigid wanted to keep the lock. But she was giving it up. Her parents couldn't return the Glass Slippers. She'd already worn them. But they could return the lock and get their money back. That might make them less annoyed.

They got to Wendy's house.

Wendy said, "Bye, Brigid. Wear your long red skirt tomorrow."

Brigid thought, I don't *have* a long red skirt.

They got to Lita's house. Lita said, "Bye, Brigid. Wear your undershirt tomorrow."

Brigid thought, Mom and Dad will say *No more fads! No undershirt!*

Brigid and Jill got to Jill's house. They stopped under the tree by the front walk.

"You can't fool me," said Jill. "You're not going to wear that red skirt tomorrow."

Uh-oh! thought Brigid. Jill knows.

"You're not going to wear your under-shirt," said Jill.

Brigid gripped the lock more tightly. Jill knew about the skirt *and* the undershirt. She must know about Maribel, too.

"I'm not?" said Brigid.

"You're going to start a new fad," said Jill. "The next fad. Can we start it together? Please?"

Brigid relaxed. Jill didn't know about Maribel. She didn't know about anything.

"*Pleeease*, Brigid?" Jill clasped her hands. "Tell me your new idea."

Brigid didn't have a new idea. But she couldn't tell Jill that.

"Wel-ll…"

Bells jingled overhead.

Brigid looked up.

Something in the tree branches stared down at her. Something the color of silver smoke.

"It's that cat!" said Jill. "The giant one we saw near your house. Remember?"

Brigid remembered, all right.

The cat jumped to the ground. It brushed against Brigid's legs. Once. Twice. Three times. Then it turned and ran down the street.

"See the bells on its collar?" said Jill. "They're the kind I wanted on my skirt."

"Really?" Brigid wasn't listening. She was watching the cat. "I have to go."

"Wait!" said Jill. "What are you wearing tomorrow?"

Brigid kept her eyes on the cat. "I haven't decided yet. I'll let you know."

Jill said, "I'll call you later."

Brigid hurried after the cat.

Brigid rounded the corner. She ran down the street. She turned another corner onto her own street.

She looked left.

She looked right.

"Up here!" called a familiar voice.

Brigid looked at the tree beside her.

Maribel sat in its branches.

"What'll I do?" Brigid wailed. "Wendy wants me to wear my long skirt. Lita wants me to wear my undershirt. Mom and Dad expect me to wear these Glass Slippers. And to use this new lock. Jill wants me to start a new fad. So does Mrs. Early."

"Great!" Maribel slid out of the tree. Her bell necklace sparkled in the sunlight. "You're the style setter. They'll like whatever you wear."

"I'm *what?*" said Brigid.

Maribel took the lock from Brigid. She spun the dial. "The style setter."

The lock sprang open.

"How did you do that?" said Brigid. "I didn't tell you the combination."

"Look at me," said Maribel.

Brigid looked.

A silver cat with golden eyes looked back at her. Its whiskers twitched and sparked.

Brigid closed her eyes and shook her head. When she opened her eyes, Maribel looked like herself again. "*Hey*," said Brigid. "How did you—?"

"Remember." Maribel slipped the lock through Brigid's belt loop. She clamped it shut. "You're the style setter. You can wear whatever you want."

Brigid blinked. She looked at the lock.

"*Whatever* I want?" she asked.

She looked up.

Maribel was gone.

That night at dinner her father said, "Brigid, you're not wearing your Cinderella shoes."

"Glass Slippers?" said Gus. He reached for another slice of pizza. "That fad is over."

Brigid's mother sighed. "We knew it wouldn't last. What's the fad now?"

"There isn't one yet," said Brigid. She slipped some pizza under the table to Badboy. "Jill wants me to start one."

"That's a good idea," said her father. "Let others follow you for a change."

Brigid looked at the lock on her belt loop. She looked at her father. "Anything I'd think of would be weird. Nobody would go along with it."

The phone rang.

"I'll get it!" said Brigid. She hurried to the hall phone and picked it up.

"Brigid, it's Jill. What's your new fad?"

Brigid looked at the lock hanging from her belt loop. She wanted to say *locks*. But she was afraid Jill would laugh at her.

"Well?" said Jill.

Brigid made up her mind. Jill wouldn't understand. No one would. Not about a lock. "I can't think of any—"

Something brushed Brigid's legs. Something soft and furry. Like a cat.

She looked down. Nothing was there. Nothing but the lock shining on her belt loop.

"Tell!" said Jill.

Brigid touched the lock. She slowly turned the dial. The clicking noise sounded. But Brigid heard another noise, too. The faint jingle of bells.

You're the style setter. Jill will like whatever you say....

Brigid said, "What would you think..."

"Yes?" said Jill.

Brigid lost her nerve. "I don't know."

The soft furry something brushed Brigid's arm.

Brigid tried again. "What would you think of...a combination lock?"

"Combination lock?" said Jill. "I don't get it."

"You wear it clamped to your belt loop." Brigid held the phone tighter. She waited for Jill to burst out laughing. She waited for her to say, *Brigid, you are so weird!*

Jill didn't say anything.

"Did you hear me?" said Brigid. "Did you—"

"Wow!" said Jill. "Great idea, Brigid! I'm putting a lock on my belt loop right now. Bye."

The line went dead.

Brigid hung up the phone. She gazed at the lock. The bells had stopped jingling. The soft furry something had stopped brushing against her.

"*Bri-gid!*" called her mother.

Brigid went back to the dining room.

"Who was on the phone?" asked her father.

"It was Jill. She wanted to know if I had a fad."

"And do you?" asked her mother.

Brigid looked from her mother to her father. She looked from Gus to Patience.

People will like whatever you do....

Brigid lifted the lock on her belt loop. "Here's my fad."

"A lock?" said Patience.

Brigid's parents rolled their eyes.

Gus hooted, "Wear that lock, and you'll be laughed out of—" He looked startled. He rubbed his cheek. "Something brushed me."

"Nonsense," said his mother. "There's nothing there." But she looked startled and rubbed her cheek.

Patience rubbed *her* cheek.

"What the—" Brigid's father rubbed his, too.

"What I started to say…That lock idea—" Gus stopped. He looked puzzled. He shrugged. "Brigid, it's great."

Her mother nodded. "Very original."

Her father smiled. "Cute."

"Can I wear a lock?" asked Patience.

Brigid couldn't believe it. She twirled the

dial. She heard the lock's deep clicking sound. She also heard a growl.

It was Badboy. Under the table. Sounding exactly as if he smelled a cat.

Don't miss the first Brigid book.

Brigid tried to straighten her knees.
She couldn't.
She tried to bend her knees further.
She couldn't do that.
She couldn't blink.
She couldn't speak.
Brigid stared down at the water.
Jump! she told herself.
She wanted to jump.
She had to jump.
She couldn't jump.

From *Brigid Bewitched*
by Kathleen Leverich

About the Author

Unlike Brigid, Kathleen Leverich never appeared in school wearing her underwear. But she did have a traumatic "undressed" experience of her own. While in costume for a first-grade play, she was sent on an errand to a *sixth*-grade classroom, clad only in a nightgown! "I think that's where it all started," she says of the idea for this book.

Kathleen Leverich is the author of several well-loved books for children, including *Best Enemies*, *Best Enemies Again*, and, of course, *Brigid Bewitched*. She lives with her husband, Walter Lorraine, in Somerville, Massachusetts.